THE TORNADO WATCHES

THE TORNADO WATCHES

An Ike and Mem Story

BY Patrick Jennings

ILLUSTRATED BY
Anna Alter

HOLIDAY HOUSE / NEW YORK

Library of Congress Cataloging-in-Publication Data
Jennings, Patrick.
The Tornado Watches / by Patrick Jennings;
illustrated by Anna Alter.—1sted.
p. cm.
"An Ike and Mem story"
Summary: A tired Ike stays up all night for four nights
to warn his family of any approaching tornadoes.
ISBN 0-8234-1672-0
[1. Tornadoes—Fiction.] I. Alter, Anna, ill. II. Title.
PZ7.J4298715 To 2002
[Fic]—dc21
2001052765

For Mom,
who watched over me
—*P. J.*

THE TORNADO WATCHES

The sky was dark after school. All the windows in Ike's house were clattering. Ike, his mother, and his little sister, Mem, were watching TV on the sofa.

"A tornado watch is in effect until eleven o'clock," the man on the TV said. There was a map behind him.

"Do we have to go down to the basement again?" Mem asked.

"Not yet," Ike answered. "So far it's just a watch. We go to the basement when it's a warning."

"That's right," Ike's mother said. She put her arms around Ike and Mem. "There's nothing to worry about."

A gray funnel cloud moved across the TV screen.

"It's kind of scary," Mem said.

Ike thought so too.

His mother squeezed them tighter.

Ike's father came home at six o'clock. He hung up his jacket.

"The radio says it's still a watch," he said.

"So does the TV," Ike's mother said. "But everything is ready in the basement. Just in case."

At seven o'clock the watch became a warning.

Ike's mother opened all the windows in the house. The wind blew all the curtains up. The windows clattered. Ike's father turned off all the lights. The room glowed with moonlight.

Ike stood at the kitchen window, looking out. The sky was filled with gray clouds. The moon behind them was full. It looked down at Ike like an eye, watching him.

"Ike!" his mother said from behind him. "Get away from that window!"

They all went down the basement steps. Ike's mother carried a candle. In the basement she lit more candles. Ike's father turned on the portable radio. He tuned it to the local station.

"A tornado warning is in effect until eight o'clock," a man on the radio said.

"I guess we'll be down here for a while," Ike's father said.

Ike's mother nodded.

Ike and Mem played Chinese checkers on a card table.

"Can a tornado carry our house away?" Mem asked Ike. "Like Dorothy and Toto's?"

Ike imagined their house flying away.

"No, sweetheart," Ike's mother said. "But a tornado can do a lot of damage. Don't worry, though. We're safe down here."

Ike could hear the windows clattering upstairs. He imagined a gray funnel cloud coming in through the front door. He imagined it going up the stairs to his room. He imagined it doing a lot of damage.

"It's your move," Mem said to him.

Ike slid a marble over to a different hole.

The warning was lifted at eight o'clock. Ike's father turned off the radio and turned on the basement light. Ike's mother blew out the candles. Then they all went upstairs. Ike's father shut all the windows.

"I think it's someone's bedtime," Ike's mother said.

It was Mem's bedtime. Ike could stay up half an hour later. He looked up *tornado* in the encyclopedia. It said that tornadoes can skip across the ground. It said that tornadoes can come day or night. It said that tornadoes can do a lot of damage.

At eight thirty Ike brushed his teeth, got into his pajamas, then climbed into bed. He lay awake on his back. He could hear the TV downstairs. If there was another tornado warning, his parents would come upstairs. Then they would all go back down to the basement. Mem wouldn't want to play Chinese checkers. She'd be too sleepy. Ike decided he should take his library book down with him.

At nine thirty Ike was still awake. He was waiting for his parents to come upstairs. He was waiting for the tornado. At ten thirty he was still waiting. The TV went off downstairs. Ike heard his parents walk to their bedroom. Their bedroom was downstairs. He heard them in their bathroom. Their bathroom was downstairs too. Then the house got very quiet.

"What if there's a tornado warning now?" Ike asked himself. "How will we know to go down to the basement?"

He climbed out of bed. He slipped on his robe and slippers. He walked to the window and looked out. All the houses in the neighborhood were dark. The sky was cloudy. The moon behind the clouds was full. It looked down at him like an eye, watching him, waiting for him—waiting for him to go to sleep.

Ike tiptoed across the hall to the playroom. He unplugged the portable TV set and carried it back to his room. He put it in his bed, under the covers, then he plugged it in and climbed

in beside it. He pulled his covers over his head and turned on the TV. He turned the volume down low.

There was an old movie on channel twelve. The movie was about a man and a woman in love. They sang songs about love. They danced. Ike watched the whole movie. Then he watched one about pirates, then one about flying saucers from another planet. He waited for the tornado warning. He waited all night.

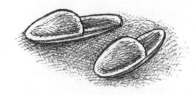

Mem came into Ike's room at seven o'clock in the morning. She saw a funny lump in his covers. She heard a funny voice.

"Ike?" she said. "Is that you?"

Ike pulled down the covers. "No," he said. "It's Captain Kangaroo."

"Why do you have the TV in bed?" Mem asked.

"Shhh!" Ike whispered. He turned off the set. "I don't want Mom and Dad to know."

He climbed out of bed and slipped on his

robe and slippers. He unplugged the TV and carried it back to the playroom. Mem followed.

"Why did you bring it to bed?" she whispered.

"Shhh!" Ike said again. He closed the playroom door. "I was watching for a tornado," he said.

Mem thought for a second. Then she asked, "Do tornadoes come out at night?"

"Uh-huh," Ike said.

Mem thought some more. Then she said, "Maybe we should sleep in the basement." She sucked her finger.

"Don't be silly," Ike said. "I'll watch out for them." He opened the door. "Go get dressed for school."

Mem went to her room and got dressed.

Ike went into the bathroom and brushed his teeth. He looked at his face in the mirror. His eyes had dark circles around them.

During math Ike set his head down on his desk for a minute and fell asleep.

"Mr. Nunn?" his teacher, Mrs. Quibble, said. "Ike?"

Ike didn't answer. He was dreaming. He dreamed a tornado was carrying Buzzy Starzinsky's swing set away. Buzzy lived next door to Ike. He was Ike's best friend.

"Ike!" Buzzy whispered. Buzzy sat next to Ike in class. "Wake up!" He leaned over and gave Ike a nudge.

Ike opened his eyes. The tornado was gone. He sat up. He was in school. He looked around the room. All the children were looking at him, and snickering.

"Mr. Nunn," Mrs. Quibble said, "we are just about to have a tornado drill. Would you care to participate?"

"Yes, ma'am," he said.

"I'm so pleased," Mrs. Quibble said. "Now remember, children," she said to the class, "when you hear the alarm, stay calm. Walk *slowly* to the door. Then walk *slowly* into the hall. Kneel down in front of your lockers, tuck your heads between your knees, and lock your hands behind your heads. Understand?"

"Yes, Mrs. Quibble," the class said.

"Fine," Mrs. Quibble said. She looked up at

the clock. It was one minute to eleven. The second hand was passing the six.

"Thirty seconds," she said.

Buzzy leaned over again toward Ike. "What's the matter with you?" he whispered. "Are you sick or something?"

Ike shook his head. "Just tired," he said.

"Did you guys go down to the basement last night?" Buzzy asked.

Ike nodded.

"Us too," Buzzy said. "Me and Mom played checkers. I beat her six times in a row."

"Twenty seconds," Mrs. Quibble said.

"You want to play checkers in the tree house after school?" Buzzy whispered.

"Sure," Ike whispered with his eyes closed.

"You sure you're not sick?" Buzzy whispered.

"Sure," Ike whispered again.

"Ten seconds," Mrs. Quibble said. "Now remember, this is only a drill. We're just practicing. There is no tornado coming."

The alarm rang. It sounded like the school bell, but it didn't stop. It kept ringing and ringing. All the children went out into the hall. They knelt down beside their lockers, tucked their heads between their knees, and locked their hands behind their heads.

Ike's locker was next to Buzzy's.

"What happens if a tornado comes at night?" Ike whispered to Buzzy. "When the TV's off?"

"Tornadoes don't come at night," Buzzy whispered.

"Yes, they do," Ike said.

"No, they don't," Buzzy said.

"Yes, they do," Ike said.

"No, they don't," Buzzy said.

The alarm stopped ringing.

"Okay, class," Mrs. Quibble said. "Good job. Please walk slowly back to your seats and take out your spelling books."

When Ike got home from school, he lay down for a minute on his bed.

His mother woke him an hour later.

"I didn't know you were lying down," she said. "Buzzy is at the door. He wants you to come out to the tree house."

"I guess I fell asleep," Ike said.

"Don't you feel well?" his mother asked. She placed the back of her hand against his forehead. "You don't feel hot."

"I'm just tired," Ike said.

His mother frowned. "I don't know," she said. "I'm going to call Dr. Baker. Maybe you should stay home from school tomorrow."

Ike almost said he was just tired again. Then he thought about staying home from school. "Okay," he said.

"I'll tell Buzzy you don't feel well," his mother said.

Later she brought Ike's supper up to him on a tray: pork chops and creamed corn. Ike fell asleep during dessert: pineapple upside-down cake. He woke up at nine o'clock that night. The tray was gone. He could hear the TV downstairs. He slipped on his robe and slippers and walked to the window. The moon was a little smaller, but it still looked like an eye, watching him, waiting for him—waiting for him to go to sleep.

Ike went back to bed. At nine thirty the TV went off downstairs. Ike heard his parents walking to their bedroom. He heard them in their bathroom. He heard the house get quiet. Then he tiptoed into the playroom and got the portable TV. When he got back, there was a funny lump in his bed. He pulled back the covers. It was Mem.

"What are you doing here?" Ike whispered.

"I don't know," Mem said. She sucked her finger.

"Well, scoot over," Ike said. He set the TV in the bed, then squeezed in between it and Mem. "Go to sleep," he whispered to her. "I'll watch."

Mem rolled over and pressed her back against Ike's. Soon she fell asleep.

Ike watched a movie about a man who bumped his head and couldn't remember anything. Then he bumped his head again and remembered. Next Ike watched a movie about Alexander Graham Bell, the man who invented the telephone. Ike thought that Bell was a good name for the man who invented the telephone. Then he watched a movie about a family with twelve children and a horse. Ike wished he had a horse.

He woke Mem up at seven.

"Better get ready for school," he told her. "I'm not walking with you today. Mom's taking you in the car. I'm going to see Dr. Baker."

"Are you sick?" Mem asked.

"I don't think so," Ike said. "But Mom thinks I might be."

Mem pouted. "I hope you're not sick," she said.

"Me too," Ike said. "But I'm not going to school."

Dr. Baker said Ike was fine. "He just needs some rest," he said to Ike's mother. He gave Ike a red sucker.

"I don't know," Ike's mother said in the car. "I still think there's something wrong." She looked at Ike. "How do you feel?" she asked.

"Okay," Ike said, yawning.

"Does your stomach hurt?"

Ike shook his head.

"Your head? Your throat?"

He shook his head twice.

"Do you feel hot? Or cold? Or achy?"

He shook it three more times.

"Well," his mother said, "I want you to stay in bed when we get home. I can move the playroom TV into your room if you want."

Ike groaned. "No, thanks," he said. "I'm really tired."

Ike slept from eleven in the morning until seven at night. He missed lunch. His mother was sitting beside him when he woke up. She had his school books in her lap.

"Buzzy dropped off your homework from Mrs. Quibble," she said. "But you don't have to do it. Not if you don't feel well."

Ike looked at his math book and his spelling book and his reading book.

"I don't feel well," he said.

"Okay," his mother said. She kissed his forehead. "Would you like something to eat? I made meat loaf for supper."

Ike smiled and nodded.

He ate the meat loaf in bed on a tray. He also ate peas and carrots and two buttered rolls. Then he ate ice cream with chocolate syrup for dessert.

"Well, your appetite is okay," his father said. He took away the tray. "Maybe tomorrow you can go to school."

"Maybe," Ike said.

Ike went to the window again that night. The moon was a little smaller. It still looked like an eye, watching him, waiting for him—waiting for him to go to sleep.

Ike waited again for his parents to go to bed. Then he tiptoed into the playroom again and got the TV. When he came back, the funny lump was back in his bed.

"Scoot over," he said.

Mem scooted over.

Ike watched a movie about a woman who

wanted to be a movie star. Then, later on, she became one. Next he watched a war movie. He had to turn down the volume. It was very noisy. Then he started watching a movie about a wolf man. The wolf man ran through a misty woods, snarling and growling. Ike changed the channel. He watched a movie about three funny guys instead.

He woke Mem up at seven.

"Are you all better now?" she asked.

Ike turned off the TV. He saw his face reflected in the screen. His eyes had dark circles around them. He felt very tired.

"I'm all better," he said.

Ike walked with Mem to school. He dropped her off in the preschool class. Then he went on to his room.

This time he fell asleep during spelling.

Mrs. Quibble called his mother. She came and got him in the car.

"I'm taking you back to Dr. Baker," she said. She looked worried.

"I'm okay, Mom," Ike said. "Really."

His mother looked at him. "Well, you don't *look* okay," she said.

Dr. Baker said Ike was fine. "He just needs some more rest," he said. He gave Ike another sucker.

"Well, what does *he* know," Ike's mother said in the car.

She took Ike home and put him to bed.

"Do you want me to bring the playroom TV in here?" she asked.

Ike groaned. "No, thanks," he said. Then he rolled over and fell asleep. He slept right through supper.

Mem came in at eight o'clock. She was wearing her pajamas. It was her bedtime.

"Ike?" she whispered. "You awake?"

Ike sat up and turned on his light. "I guess so," he said.

Mem ran across the floor and jumped up on his bed. She bounced up and down on it.

"Are you going to watch for tornadoes tonight?" she whispered as she bounced.

"Uh-huh," Ike said, yawning. "But that's a secret. Okay?"

"Cross my heart and hope to die, stick a needle in my eye," Mem said, and crossed her heart and pretended to stick a needle in her eye. Then she did a sit-jump, a knee-jump, and a stop-jump.

"Can I come in later again?" she whispered.

Ike sighed. "Sure," he said.

Mem jumped down from the bed and ran off to her room.

Ike slipped on his robe and slippers and went to the window. The moon was even smaller. It still looked like an eye. It still watched him. It still waited.

Ike stayed up later than his parents again. He went and got the playroom TV again. There was a lump under the covers again.

"Scoot over," he said.

Mem scooted over.

Ike watched a movie about a cowboy. The cowboy put his guns away forever. Then, later on, he got them out again. Next Ike watched a movie about a different cowboy. This cowboy fell in love with an Indian maiden. Everyone was mad at him—everyone except the Indian maiden. Then Ike started watching a movie about a circus clown with a terrible secret, but he never found out the secret. He fell asleep.

When Ike awoke, he heard windows clattering. He had never heard windows clatter so much. He also heard sirens and the portable radio.

"I repeat," the man on the radio said, "a tornado warning is now in effect until one A.M."

"Mom?" Ike said, sitting up. He looked around. He was in the basement.

"I'm right here," Ike's mother said. She sat down beside him on his cot. "It's okay. We're in the basement. I carried you down. There's a tornado warning."

"A tornado?" Ike said. "How did you know? Were you watching TV?"

"No," Ike's mother said with a smile. "The wind woke us. Then we heard the sirens."

Ike looked at Mem's cot. She was in it, sleeping. She was hugging her stuffed bunny, Gina. Ike's father was sitting in a chair beside her, sleeping. He had a book in his lap. It was Mem's picture book about the circus.

Ike remembered the movie about the clown with the terrible secret.

"I fell asleep," he said.

"It's late," Ike's mother said. She eased Ike back onto the cot. "Go back to sleep."

Ike closed his eyes, but he couldn't sleep. He listened to the radio. He listened to the siren. He listened to the wind. It got louder and louder. His ears popped. Ike felt as if he were on an airplane.

"It's close," Ike heard his father say.

Ike opened his eyes.

Mem woke up and began to cry. "My ears hurt!" she said.

Ike's father lifted her onto his lap. Mem cried into his robe.

Then suddenly there was a very loud sound. It was louder than the wind and the windows and the siren. It went *BOOM!*—like an explosion on TV.

"What was *that?*" Ike's father said. His eyes looked a little scared. So Ike felt scared. Mem cried harder.

"We're okay," Ike's mother said. "We're okay."

And then, little by little, the house got quieter. The siren stopped sounding. The windows stopped clattering. The wind stopped howling.

Mem fell asleep. But Ike couldn't. He sat up in his cot and read Mem's picture book. His library book was up in his room.

Then a bell started ringing. It rang and rang. It was the doorbell.

Ike and his mother and father climbed the stairs. His mother carried Mem. She was still sleeping.

Ike's mother flicked the kitchen light switch on. The kitchen stayed dark. "The power's out," she said.

Ike looked out the kitchen window. The sky was pitch-black. There were no clouds. There was no moon.

Ike's mother went into the living room and set Mem down on the sofa. Ike's father flicked on the switch for the porch light. The porch stayed dark. Ike's father flicked the switch on and off and on and off.

"The power's out," Ike's mother said again.

"I forgot," Ike's father said.

He turned the knob and opened the door. Buzzy Starzinsky and his mother and father were standing on the stoop. Buzzy's mother was crying. Ike had never seen her cry before.

"It's our house!" she sobbed.

Ike's mother put her arm around Buzzy's mother. "Come on in," she said.

"The wind took the roof right off!" Buzzy's father said. He shook his head. "Thank heavens we were down in the basement!"

"Well, you stay here tonight," Ike's father said. He patted Buzzy's father on the shoulder. "We'll take care of everything tomorrow. You'll see."

Ike looked at Buzzy. He had dark circles around his eyes.

"You were right," Buzzy said. "They come at night."

Buzzy slept in Ike's bed with Ike. Buzzy slept with his head at the foot of the bed so they could fit. His parents slept on the cots in the playroom. Mem slept downstairs with her mother and father.

In the morning Ike's family and Buzzy's family had breakfast together: scrambled eggs and sausage. They couldn't have toast. The power was still out.

Ike and Mem and Buzzy didn't have to go to school after breakfast. It was Saturday.

Instead they and their parents went next door to Buzzy's house. They stood in the front yard and looked at the big hole in Buzzy's roof. There was a lot of stuff on the lawn. Some of it was from Buzzy's house. Some of it wasn't. Buzzy's mother picked up an old stuffed bear.

"It's Reuben," she said to Buzzy.

Buzzy took it quickly, then hid it behind his back.

"Luckily, the tornado just skipped over our place," Buzzy's father said. "But it touched down over on Poplar Avenue and completely wrecked the Browns' place."

"Oh, how awful for Jean and Burt!" Ike's mother said. "We'll have to go over there later."

Ike's father nodded.

Buzzy's mother began to cry again. "At least we're all okay," she sobbed.

"That's right," Ike's mother said. She put her arm around her. "That's the important thing."

Then they all walked around to the backyard. Buzzy's swing set was still there, but the tree in Ike's backyard had been knocked over. It was stuck in the phone lines. Ike and Buzzy's tree house was in the street, in pieces.

"Our tree house!" Buzzy said. He started to run over to it, but his father stopped him.

"It's not safe over there," Buzzy's father said. "The lines are down."

"I'd better go in and call the fire department," Ike's father said. He walked away toward the house.

Ike's mother put her hand on Ike's shoulder. "I'm sorry about your tree house," she said.

Mem leaned her head against Ike's arm. "It's a good thing you were watching the TV for tornadoes," she said.

Ike looked up at his mother. She was smiling.

"I fell asleep," Ike said to Mem. "Other people are watching."

A fire truck pulled into Ike's driveway. Some fire fighters lifted the tree out of the phone lines. They set the pieces of the tree house in Ike's backyard. Ike and Buzzy picked through them. They found their ceremonial candle. They found Buzzy's ceremonial cape. They couldn't find Ike's. They found their top secret tree house code box.

All the roofers in town were very busy that day. None of them could come to fix Buzzy's roof. Ike's father and Buzzy's father climbed up on ladders and covered the hole with a tarp.

"You stay with us until it's fixed," Ike's mother told Buzzy's mother.

Buzzy's mother nodded and sniffled.

That night they all had supper together in the dining room. They ate by candlelight. The power was still out.

After dinner Ike and Mem and Buzzy did the dishes. Then they played Chinese checkers on the floor in the living room. The grown-ups played cribbage on the card table. Then, suddenly, the porch light came on outside.

"The power!" Ike's mother said. She turned on the lamps in the living room and blew out the candles. She didn't turn on the TV.

At eight o'clock Mem went to bed. Ike and

Buzzy went up to Ike's room and worked on some new secret codes. At eight thirty Ike's father came up.

"Lights out, boys," he said.

Ike and Buzzy got into their pajamas and climbed into bed. Buzzy lay with his head at the foot again.

"My mom says we can't build a new tree house in the yard," Ike whispered. "None of the trees left are strong enough to hold one."

Buzzy didn't answer.

"Buzzy?" Ike whispered. He sat up. Buzzy was already asleep. Reuben was tucked against his chest.

Ike lay back on the bed. At ten thirty he heard his parents walk to their bedroom. He heard them in their bathroom. He heard

Buzzy's parents coming up the stairs. He heard them in the upstairs bathroom. Then he heard them walk to the playroom. He heard them shut the playroom door. He couldn't get the TV now if he wanted to.

He didn't want to.

He climbed out of bed and went to the window. All the houses in the neighborhood were dark. There were no clouds in the sky. The moon was up. It was smaller still. It still looked like an eye. A tired one.

Ike climbed back into bed with Buzzy and soon fell asleep.

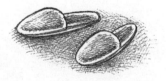